The Warren

ALSO BY BRIAN EVENSON

NOVELS

Dark Property

Father of Lies

Last Days

Immobility

COLLECTIONS

Altmann's Tongue

The Din of Celestial Birds

The Wavering Knife

The Open Curtain

Fugue State

Windeye

A Collapse of Horses

AS B. K. EVENSON

Aliens: No Exit

Dead Space: Martyr

Dead Space: Catalyst

THE WARREN

BRIAN EVENSON

A TOM DOHERTY ASSOCIATES BOOK
NEW YORK

This is a work of fiction. All of the characters, organizations, and events portrayed in this novella are either products of the author's imagination or are used fictitiously.

THE WARREN

Copyright © 2016 by Brian Evenson

Cover art by Victor Mosquera
Cover design by Christine Foltzer

Edited by Ann VanderMeer

All rights reserved.

A Tor.com Book
Published by Tom Doherty Associates
175 Fifth Avenue
New York, NY 10010

www.tor.com

Tor® is a registered trademark of Macmillan Publishing Group, LLC

ISBN 978-0-7653-9314-2 (ebook)
ISBN 978-0-7653-9315-9 (trade paperback)

First Edition: September 2016

P1

for Gene Wolfe

I

I shall begin this written record by reporting the substance of our last conversation—which was not only the last conversation I had with Horak but the last I had with anyone or ever expect to have. Perhaps the last conversation that any two humans will have, if he and I can be said to both qualify as human. There is apparently some debate on that score. Or would be if he had not abandoned me. Was some debate, I should say.

I did not know how to make the machine function properly, and did not know either how to shut it off—it was not me who suspended him within the machine in the first place. The instructions for the operation of the machine were to be found in a sector that proved to be decayed, the data irretrievable. Nor did I know the sequence or the code, and my slow muddlings got me nowhere. In the end, seeing my own time ticking away with nothing resolved, I decided drastic measures were justified.

• • •

How long has it been since a person left the warren and how long did he survive? I had asked the monitor earlier, before all this. I knew the answer to this question: the last of us to leave the warren had left one hundred and forty days ago—I wanted to see if the monitor knew this fact or if this portion of the data was also corrupted. The last of us to leave was named Wollem, a name chosen for him by the pair who had come before him, Vigus and Vagus. When they neared the end of their lives, they had themselves imprinted within the monitor and then set about constructing Wollem. They had hoped to make a pair, as had always been done before, but there was so little material that out of prudence they opted to make only one, so that he in turn could make another one, so there might be at least a little more time given to us before a final end. One hundred and forty days ago, Wollem left in search of more material, knowing he would die in the process. But, with luck, he would die only after returning with sufficient material for others to be formed and for us to persist a while longer.

He did not return.

To my question, the monitor responded: *Query: what do you mean by person?*

I thought about this a long time and then asked, "What do *you* mean by person?"

It responded, *Bipedal, an individual thought process en-*

meshed in a body, procreated through the fertilization of an ovum by a sperm and its subsequent development in a womb.

"Only the first criterion is relevant."

With this definitional clarification, it said, *this sort of "person" left one hundred and forty days ago. He did not return. It is not known how long he survived. This is not a question for which there is sufficient data to provide an answer.*

"Is it likely he survived?"

It is not likely.

"And if all three criteria are considered relevant?" I asked.

By these criteria, it has been seventy-one years, eleven months, six days, and twenty-one hours since a person left the warren. He still survives and has been carefully preserved.

• • •

But I intended to start differently. I allowed myself to get distracted. Since I learned most things in a way that I have come to feel would not be considered normal for those who might read this record, my sense of balance and order is sometimes far from perfect. At times, I become confused about the order in which things should be told. Parts of me know things that other parts do not, and sometimes I both know a thing and do not know it, or part of me knows something is true and another part knows it is not true, and there is nothing to allow me to negotiate between the two. The monitor can help if I ask the right questions, but in many circumstances it just adds another layer of confusion so that whatever is being choked or stifled is even more so.

"He still survives?" I asked.

Yes, said the monitor.

"Does he have a name?"

Yes. Horak.

"He has been preserved?" I asked. "On an impression?"

Not on an impression. Being preserved on an impression is not the same thing as being alive. His body has been physically stored and his mind along with it.

"Show me where."

It showed me a schematic. Horak was, in fact, quite close. Perhaps through some of the tunnels of the warren that had been filled, he could be reached, I thought at first, but then another self within me stirred, opened its pale eye, and said, *No, on the surface.*

"Is he outside?" I asked myself.

He is in a facility. Don't you remember?

"No," I said.

I do, it said. I said.

"Is the facility at"—eye after eye opened within me as I groped for a word, finally found it—"ground level?"

Yes.

"And he's still alive?" I asked, amazed.

• • •

Some of the sectors pertaining to the proper use of a suit had been corrupted, but not all of them. As a result, I had some information and some noise, and needed only to determine what was information and what was noise, and then determine which parts of me I should ignore and which I should listen to. Could I survive at ground level? Yes, it was clear, but not for long. Longer if I was wearing a suit, but even then not long. How long was *not long*? The answer to this question was unclear, and querying the monitor did little good. *No sensors currently accessible at ground level,* it indicated, and then seemed to consider the matter closed.

• • •

After Wollem had formed me and made it possible for me to communicate, and then imbued me with the further quickening that made me a receptacle for the selves that had come before me, he told me: *My purpose is complete. Now I go in search of help.* I am almost certain that I remember him saying this. And that after saying it, he drew a suit up around his body, sealed it, and left the warren.

After he departed, I lay there on my tablature, for how long I do not know. I was trying to translate the vast amount of damaged and partial information that had been poured into my mind into some sort of rational order, into something useful. I could see, in vivid detail, the means by which a finger could be made to flex and move—I understood the electrical impulse that would best bring this about but seemed unable to manifest it. I do not know how long I lay spread on the tablature, trying to move a single finger. And then, suddenly, I did manage a pulse of electricity and the finger moved. But when I examined what I had in my head again, I saw the simple movement of a finger had burnt a line there, a minuscule thread, hardly noticeable unless you happened to be looking for it, unless you happened to be looking very closely because you needed something very specific and saw the way that the line split that thing in two and even obliterated the slightest portion of it. And then I understood that everything I said, everything I did, would do damage to whatever was already contained within me, that there was hardly enough space in my head for all the various selves, let alone their memories, let alone my own.

What did I do? For a long time I did not move, waiting

to see if what I held within my head would congeal in some way, become resistant or formalized or . . . I don't know. I could see how the information that was there was part of different strata, that what I had thought upon waking was just one being was in fact many layered one atop the other, that I was the partial record of all those who had come before me. These I began to peel off, divide up, and put to sleep, so that I could keep them straight and, if possible, safe.

But in the end I could only do so much of this. In the end, I had no choice but to move another finger.

• • •

Wollem came back into the room wearing a suit, prepared to leave, to go to ground level. Or rather, no, that was not what it felt like at the time. I am not sure this is my true memory or instead the memory of an earlier self. At the time, whether my memory or another's, what it felt like was this: Wollem left the room. He was gone for a time. I struggled to move a finger and began to rearrange the architecture of my mind. And then a figure, bipedal but featureless, made of vulcanized cloth, with a head made of a bulb of steel and tempered glass, entered the room and spoke in a tinny voice. The figure waved once and then was gone. It was only later that I stumbled upon a sector on the monitor that told me this was a man wearing a suit. This man must have been, so I deduced since there was nobody else, Wollem.

• • •

I rummaged through the warren until I found a suit that reminded me of that suit I had seen, and then I forced my body into it. There were cracks and splits in it, a rent in the stomach, the fabric stained around it by what looked like rust. *Doesn't matter if there are holes,* part of me that was still awake thought, *you're dead anyway if you go outside.*

But I opened up each pale eye within me and inquired until I found enough to tell me to rummage some more, and then I tried to close all the eyes again at once, to seal each back—for their own good, for their safety. Each was already crisscrossed with darkness and scars and damage, and awakening them seemed only to damage them worse, so better to keep them asleep.

I rummaged until I found a rusted can of sealant—though the rust on the can was of a somewhat different color than that on the lips of the tear in the suit. Perhaps merely a difference in material. I shook it and sprayed it. When it came out and I positioned it correctly, it bubbled and filled the cracks and splits, and sealed the lips of the rent not only to one another but to my skin beneath, so thoroughly that to remove it later I had to take a knife to my belly and separate a strip of skin from my body.

• • •

Wollem told me: "I was taught by Vigus and Vagus in a different way than you will be. Some things were imprinted, but only the most basic of things and with gaps between. The ability to chew and swallow, the ability to walk and crawl, the basics of language. Then Vigus and Vagus took turns instructing me. Once they were gone, I learned from the monitor.

"But the monitor is not what it was. Whole sectors are damaged. Vigus's personality is still preserved, but Vagus's is so damaged that if he were to be brought back, he would be mad. For years we fooled ourselves into thinking we could preserve ourselves in such fashion and be reconstituted later when someone came to relieve us. But no one is coming. No one ever will come, unless it will be someone who means us harm."

• • •

And yet, even knowing this, even believing this as he did,

once he had imprinted me not just with simple gestures and abilities but with the surviving personalities of our expedition, Wollem could not stop himself from going out to look for someone or something to save us.

• • •

There are times when I look back at this writing and do not recognize what I have written. There are moments, whole pages even, that are written in my hand, to be sure, but that I have no memory of writing. When I awake, I sometimes find myself deep in the warren before the writing desk, with the charcoal grasped tight in my hand and no memory of how I arrived there.

I am writing this on paper even though such writing is a forgotten art. I am writing on paper because I have seen the way that sectors of the monitor and other recording devices can become corrupted and whole selves, as a result, are lost. I am trying to leave behind a record that will survive. Apparently, judging from the passages that I do not remember but that are nonetheless written, I am not the only part of me doing this.

• • •

I do not have an earliest memory. All the memories came

at once, an overlay of a dozen different personalities and all the memories going along with them. Or at least some of the memories—there is not enough room and each new memory I make, each new thing I do, ends up sacrificing memories that came before. Each moment I live snuffs out a little more of the lives of the others within me.

Wollem meant well. When he discovered what was happening within the monitor, the fact that the majority of personalities imprinted within the monitor had grown corrupt with time, he did not know what else to do. He could have let each recorded personality lapse, could have waited until, one after another, they either grew corrupt or the monitor or the tablature broke down sufficiently so as to make organic reinscription of these personalities possible. Instead, having one last source of material at his disposal, he formed me, and then, within me, formed everyone who remained.

And yet, Wollem did not inscribe his own personality. He did not reproduce himself either on the monitor or, organically, within my brain, along with the dozen or so others. Why? Was it merely an oversight on his part? Was it because he knew there were already too many within me? Or was it selfishness, a very real desire to let his flesh and self die together, to keep his self to himself?

• • •

Suit affixed, heart pounding, I squirreled my way along the edges of the warren and came to the first seal. This was much farther than I had ever gone before. I removed the seal and ignored the warning sirens. I had salvaged a piece of rebar from the failed portion of the warren, the damaged portion, and positioned it to keep the seal open, just in case it was inclined to slide closed while I was gone or in case, despite the damage the warren had undergone, there was some mechanism that would, after a certain amount of time had passed, draw the seal closed.

I climbed the ladder, slowly, putting one foot over the other as I had been taught to do. As I did so, I felt several pairs of eyes within my head flicker open, awakened by a movement that was familiar to them, from their own climbs to the surface many years before. The strangeness of that: the feeling that you, or rather I, are at once dreaming and remembering and simultaneously doing something as if for the first time. That terrible rapid construction of the world around you, but not as a new world; instead, as a world already known, already seen. At the top of the ladder was a second seal. I had not known I would encounter it until my hand reached out in the dim and touched it, but once touched it sprang forth fully formed. A set of eyes within my head opened, but another set opened wider, and I climbed down the ladder and found a second piece of rebar and then climbed back up again.

It was difficult to force open this second seal. I had to pound on it with the piece of rebar, and as I did so, flakes of rust sifted slowly down around me and adhered to my faceplate, mottling my vision. At first, I thought it was not going to open for me, and then a voice from a self within me directed me how to brace the rebar and use it as a lever and, by so doing, slowly force the seal open. Even then the seal did not give until, abruptly, it did and I lost my hold and dropped the bar clattering down the shaft and almost tumbled down myself.

Light, the shock of it, more searing and intense than anything I'd ever seen. Then, blind, I was up and through the seal and on the surface, up and running now, all the eyes of the selves I harbor in my head open now and the mouths attached to them counting a measured cadence, *one one thousand, two one thousand, three one thousand,* and on and on, the numbers growing, the heads within my head growing anxious and me myself anxious along with them. How much time, in the suit, did I have before we would be poisoned and die? And then I had scampered across the bare, damaged ground and was at the seal of the facility, wondering with a sinking feeling if I should have brought another piece of rebar. I stumbled into the wall and applied the palm of my glove to the pressure pad, and, unexpectedly, the door slid open and I tumbled into a solitary room.

Within, it was the same as the warren—the same, rather, as the farthest walls of the warren, without the modifications that we had developed over the years. So much so that I became quickly convinced that this was part of the warren or once had been.

The storage unit occupied the center of the room, humming slightly, cables running up into the ceiling. It was as tall as my chest and twice as thick as a man, rooted solidly in the floor. Inside was a figure, human or nearly so. Crystals of ice were in his hair and he was frozen.

"Monitor," I asked the room at large, "are you here as well?"

There was no answer. I looked for a monitor port but there was no port, so perhaps this had never been part of the warren after all.

The eyes within my head had stopped rolling now, had begun to calm, lids growing heavy, even beginning, in some cases, to drowse. I reached up to remove the helmet from my suit, making the motions exaggerated and definite, and though several stirred within me, when they became cognizant of what I was about to do and where I was, they lulled again. This, coupled with the green light now burning above the door, I took as an indication that it was safe, that I could breathe and not die.

• • •

As I have said, parts of me are damaged, and so are the records we have that are stored in the monitor. I know more than most who came before me, but they had the advantage of having access to memories recorded outside of themselves, in the monitor. With those systems working, they could in an instant learn things that I cannot and never will. For me, memory is not only at times flawed and corrupted but also overlapped and confused, one personality hiding parts of another, blending too, so that the selves within my head sometimes seem many-headed and monstrous or deformed and impossible to comprehend.

I kept touching parts of the storage machine, thinking that the gestures would reveal something to me, would awaken someone within me, a self that would know what to do.

But nothing happened.

I took my suit off—or would have if I had not fused it to my skin while sealing the rip. I wriggled my arms free and let the suit hang around my waist, tugging at my belly. Hands freed, I touched the controls and the pad of the storage unit with my bare fingers, thinking it might respond to my touch or my heat, but it did not respond at all.

For nearly a day I was there, trying to make something happen. Nothing happened. At last, in frustration, nothing accomplished, I donned the suit again, opened the seal, and made a mad dash back to the warren.

• • •

"Monitor," I asked, immediately upon my return, "when did the last person go out and when did he return?"

Query: what do you mean by person? it asked.

"As before. Bipedal," I said. "None of the other qualifications."

The last person to go out went out fourteen hours and forty-six minutes ago. He returned eight minutes ago. You are that person.

• • •

"Monitor," I asked, "is the storage facility that keeps Horak part of the warren?"

Query: what do you mean by warren? it asked.

"This place," I said. "What you see all around you."

For a long moment, the monitor did not respond, and

I thought that it had at last reached its point of exhaustion. Everything is running down, dying. *Perhaps the monitor will not outlast you,* I thought. *Perhaps, before you die, you will lose even that small consolation.*

And then the monitor said, *No. It is on the surface. This place is not on the surface.*

"The warren," I said.

If you call it that.

"But were they once connected?" I persisted.

Everything was once connected, responded the monitor. *Everything still is.*

I called up all the files related to storage. There was nothing that could be seen, nothing that could be read, nothing more than a few bits and pieces of code, a fragmented, damaged hodgepodge that told me nothing.

• • •

I could tell you how I tried to awaken him and how it all failed. But I have not even succeeded in telling you what I planned to begin with, and there is no point, or little point, in pushing that goal even farther away on the horizon by stacking more and more up in front of it. No, it is enough to say that I, or *we* if you prefer, failed. We could not start the mechanism to unstore this Horak. It had been done before, I knew it had been done, but there was no record of it anywhere, not even fragments. It was as if this part of our history had been wiped deliberately and mercilessly away.

Is there a reason for this? an awakening part of me wondered. *Do I really know what I am getting into?*

I knew something of this Horak from my earlier conversation with the monitor. He apparently was not constructed but rather procreated through the fertilization of an ovum by a sperm and its subsequent development in a womb. He was, according to the monitor, an individual thought process enmeshed solitarily within a body. It is thought, at least by some residing within me, that unlike us he could not be hurt by being outside. There were some within me who felt he was not human, though others argued that he was a true human, a first human, whom we all had been set to emulate. Others still thought he had once been human but had, due to circumstances, changed.

What was true and what was rumor, it was difficult to say: it is impossible for me to be objective about the opinions of all the selves contained within me, for I hear not only their words but feel along with them the weight of their conviction.

Better to be cautious, to wait and see if I can figure a way to awaken him, and if I cannot, perhaps I can convince myself that it is better not to awaken him at all.

And so, knowing all this, believing all this, I removed the suit and tore my strip of flesh off along with it, then bandaged my belly, ate, and fell asleep, trusting that tomorrow was another day, that tomorrow anything could happen.

• • •

And yet, when I awoke, it was to find myself fully clothed in the suit with no memory of having dressed myself. I was not in the warren but rather in the facility above ground. I was, I was shocked to discover, standing beside the storage tank and had in my hand a device for the cutting of metal pipes. With it, I saw, I had severed the cables running along the back of Horak's tank. Alarms were blaring and all the eyes within me had sprung open, and the machine before me had begun to thaw, water condensing all along its surface.

Who is it that awakens when I sleep to take control of my body? What do they want? I turned my gaze inward and scrutinized the eyes I saw, but nothing was revealed to me. So I turned my eyes back around and stared outward, at the tank.

I thought, *This will kill him.*

And then I thought, *No. If he is as they say, perhaps he will survive it. We can only watch and wait.*

II

When he first was removed, he was dead, I was sure of it. The thaw had been improper and more than enough to kill him. His skin had turned black in places and was suppurating in others.

I squatted over his corpse, staring down at it, wondering what to do. Perhaps I would simply drag it outside and leave it there, in the open air, to decay. There were, according to the monitor, no animals or insects, no bacteria even. The corpse would remain there, perhaps for decades, slowly mummifying.

And then the dead body took a deep, juddering breath and proved itself alive.

• • •

For many hours, days even, he shivered and shook. He lay there, hardly able to breathe or move, his eyes opening occasionally to look desperately around him. I stayed beside him. At a certain point, I descended back into the warren and returned with some food and water and tried to give them to him, but he would not part his lips to receive them, and I could not force them on him out of fear that he might choke. Several times he tried to say something, his voice barely above a whisper, but by the time I had brought my ear down close enough to hear him, he had finished and did not repeat it.

Twice I awoke to find my hands clenched around his throat, some other personality within me having taken charge of the body as I slept, and the second time my thumbs left black marks on the throat and his tongue lolled out as if he were dead again, and I believe that for a time he was indeed again dead. But then came again that same awful juddering breath as he either barely clung to life or came back from the dead.

He did not die for good, and yet he got no better. He lingered on a threshold between life and death. I was a danger to him, I knew—or not I exactly, but one of those others imprinted within me—which is, in a sense, both the same and not.

And yet, who am I to say that the person I think I am, the personality that had risen to the top like cream, is the real me? These others fill up more of me than I do. Perhaps one of them is the real me and I am the interloper.

• • •

Thoughts such as these—considered as I sat beside Horak, waiting for his final breath and then, when it came, his next final breath, and the one that came after that—led me into darker speculations. What was I, I could not help but think, but a repository, a refuge for souls without bodies? Here, before me, was a soul with a fatally damaged body, a soul that could not stay in life and yet could not flee. He was not the same as the rest of us, but there was room for him. We would have him imprinted and then I would take the imprinting into myself and then, together, we would continue.

Which was why I affixed my faceplate again, shrugged my way back into my suit, and, grabbing him by the arms, prepared to drag him to the warren to have the monitor inscribe him onto me.

• • •

There were, as it turned out, problems I had not foreseen. I brought Horak out into the open air above ground, thinking that this alone might kill him, but he kept breathing. Grunting and sweating, I dragged him across the baked and dusty ground and toward the seal leading down to the access ladder. But as I got there, I realized I did not have the strength to carry him down the ladder. I could not drop him down the shaft—the fall would break his neck and no doubt kill him. I had to figure out some way to get him down.

Rope, I thought. I use the term *I* loosely, of course. Better to say, *Rope, he thought, and I listened.*

I descended the ladder and passed through the seal at the bottom and then rooted through the warren until I found, half buried behind a stack of cement blocks, a dusty coil of rope. It was long enough, or close enough to being so that, if he had to fall the last few feet, he might do so with little risk of injury. It was sturdy, or seemed so. Sturdy enough, I hoped.

I slung it over my shoulder and climbed back up the ladder.

As I pushed my head through the second seal, I saw that in my absence he had rolled over on his side and turned slightly toward me. His eyes were open. His mouth was in a tight line and I could see his hands twitching. And then, seeing him opening his mouth and struggling to speak, I bent closer, brought the receptive port of my helmet very close to his mouth.

"Leave me," Horak whispered.

"There's no point in leaving you," I reasoned. "I'll bring you below. We'll imprint you and then, even if your body does not survive, you shall survive within me."

His head made a brief palsied movement, which might have been involuntary or might have been a denial. I came a few steps higher on the ladder and began to affix the rope around him. But when he realized what I was doing, he scrabbled weakly at the rope, trying to push it away.

"Stay," he whispered again, "stay here."

"It's dangerous here," I told him. "Poison. It'll kill you. We need to take you below."

"No," Horak whispered.

I hesitated a moment and then ignored him, continued to construct a harness around him by which I could lower him into the warren. It was nearly complete when I felt a pain in my side and saw that, despite his incapacitation, he had managed to produce a knife from somewhere and force it through the fabric of my suit until it penetrated my skin. As I reached for it, he drew it down, shallowly wounding me and tearing a large rent in the fabric.

All the eyes within me shuddered open at once and I found myself riding on a swell of panic. I pulled away and the knife slid cleanly out and then he whispered something that I did not understand and the knife slipped from his hand and fell with a thud into the dirt beside his head. A part of me, the part that I will refer to as the real me, wanted to stay and finish the job, to complete the harness and lower Horak into the warren. But the other mouths within my skull were counting now, their panic slowly rising, counting quickly away the moments I had left to live. And so I left him there and passed through the outer seal and clattered down the ladder and slid through the inner seal and then stripped off the suit itself and saw my side stained with my own flavescent blood and began to vomit, though whether from the shock of seeing my own condition or from being exposed to the poison of the outside air, I still cannot say. Perhaps a little of both.

• • •

I would not rise to the surface to check on Horak, I told myself. He did not want my help, I owed him nothing, better to leave him to die there. No, I told myself, I would waste no more time on him.

And yet there were other parts of me, other bits that whispered, *Climb the ladder,* and these voices grew louder within me, harder and harder to resist. In the end what could I do but climb?

He was there still, just where I had left him, the knife lying in the dirt beside him, the tip stained with my blood. He was, as far as I could gather, still alive. Or perhaps alive again. It was impossible for me to be sure on that score. His body, the damaged portions in particular, had become filmed with a milky weblike substance, as if a cocoon were forming around him, and through the surface of this web I could see a regular pulsing of dark fluid that it took me some moments of staring to realize was something akin to blood. His own blood, if the pallor of the flesh beneath was any indication.

I did not understand what was happening to him, and whether it was something brought about by his own body or by something exterior to him. There was nothing within or outside of me, in pure or damaged form, to give me any hint or indication. Was it a good thing or a bad thing? All I knew was that watching it terrified me.

I did not dare touch him. I regretted having climbed the ladder. I slid back through the aperture of the seal and climbed down and promised myself that I would not return.

• • •

The days proceeded as they had before Horak. I grew older, hour by hour, and extinction drew closer. I continued my record, making notes with charcoal and paper that would be left in case someone did outlast me. I searched the warren for anything we had missed, any materials that might be used to form a descendant, and found nothing. I scoured the remaining fragmented archives and consulted the monitor, hoping to find some indication of where such materials might be found within a range that I might have a chance of successfully retrieving them and repropagating myself rather than succumbing to extinction. Had there been anything, even the hope of anything, I would have donned the suit and stepped through the seal and over the enshrouded body of Horak and gone to find it. But there was no such indication, and I had no idea where to start. Better, I told myself, to keep scouring the warren, keep scouring the knowledge of the personalities within my skull, keep searching for the question that when asked properly to the monitor would reveal a possibility of continuance. But better or no, I still found nothing.

• • •

It might have gone on like this for some time, perhaps even forever: the doddering torpor of an aging person, if I could be said to fit the proper definition of person, as he approaches an extinction not just personal but extending to his entire species. I could have let my life dribble away like that, not knowing what else to do. And, indeed, would have, had I been left alone.

But I was not left alone. I was never alone. How could I be left alone, considering the number of selves that had been inscribed on the surface of my brain?

• • •

I awoke on the ladder, wearing the suit. How I had gotten there, I did not know. All the eyes still left intact within me seemed open, none of them accepting blame. Was I on my way outside, or had I been outside already? I had no way of knowing. There was a moment in which I considered climbing out to see what was on the other side, to examine the state of Horak's body, and there were parts of me that leapt at the possibility, but other parts recoiled. I made my way back down the ladder and secured the suit within a storage chest, and then locked the chest and secured the key.

• • •

"Monitor," I inquired, trying to learn how far I had gone, "when did the last person go outside and when did he return?"

Question disabled, said the monitor.

"What do you mean, 'question disabled'?"

The question cannot be answered without the proper employment of a password.

"Who told you that you were not allowed to answer the question?"

You did.

"It was not me," I said.

The monitor did not respond.

"Answer the question," I said.

The question cannot be answered without the proper employment of a password.

"I established the password," I said. "I should be allowed to remove it. Monitor, there is no longer a password."

The monitor did not respond.

"Monitor," I said, "when did the last person go outside and when did he return?"

Question disabled. System shutting down.

• • •

I awoke a second time on the ladder, and this time without the suit, naked and shivering, on my way up to the outside world, unless I had already been outside—but no, that wasn't possible: had I been I would now be sick or dead.

I am working against myself. There are parts of me ready to betray me, and I no longer have clear control over them, particularly when I sleep. If I am not careful, I will fall asleep and when I wake up I will not be the self that is currently spread over the body like sweat, touching all parts of it, but one of the selves held close within the skull of the body, locked inside.

III

For a few days, I was fine. Nothing happened, or nothing seemed to. I was, at least, still alive, not sick, and the suit remained locked in the storage chest, so I had not been outside, at least not for long. I was lonely for the voice of the monitor, but there are, if I am to be honest with myself, enough voices as it is. The loss of one, even that of the monitor, is something I can survive. I was beginning to relax. Hope had begun to return. I would find something, I told myself. There was something buried in the dirt of the closed portions of the tunnel, or some bit of uncorrupted knowledge that when uncovered would allow us to continue, for us to persist until the air became such that we could survive it and participate in a different kind of life, for us to persist until there would be no need for external material to fashion us, where the thought processes enmeshed in a body would be singular rather than multiple, and the answer to all three of the monitor's initial qualifications for personhood would be met.

• • •

I fell asleep thinking such utopian thoughts. There were dreams, but they were muddled, shot through with shadow.

When I awoke, I knew something was wrong. For a moment, I did not recognize my surroundings and thought I must have ascended the ladder again or, at the very least, moved from one portion of the warren to another. But no, I was on my cot, in my room. My arms I had flung back and over my head. During the night, they had slipped over the edge of the cot; they tingled now as if they did not have sufficient blood. My neck, too, had become bent and was now stiff. It was only in forcing it to turn that I realized someone else was in the room, hanging over me in the darkness, motionless, watching.

For a moment, I felt as though one of the selves inside me had been extruded out of my mouth and had taken on physical form. And then the figure, noting my eyes were open, moved, and I saw that it was Horak.

He looked haggard and ill, but his skin had healed, the necrosis of the flesh having vanished. There were still, here and there, little scraps of webbing, as if he had only recently broken from a cocoon.

"You're alive," I said.

He did not reply. Perhaps he saw no reason to reply.

"How did you get in here?" I asked.

"I came in," he simply said.

"How did you pass through the seals?"

He held out his hand and pressed it to my chest, and I felt unnatural warmth to it. "Shh," he said. "Just relax. Sleep." Even when he removed his hand, my chest still felt warm where he had touched me.

But I could not sleep. *Perhaps I am asleep already,* I thought, and bit the inside of my mouth, but the pain did not wake me. If I was asleep, I could not know it, might never know it. For a moment I kept my eyes closed, and then I opened them. Horak was still there, hanging over me, just as, perhaps, frozen, he had hung for years in storage.

• • •

I slid up in the bed until I was sitting. Horak did not try to stop me this time, but he observed me as I did so, his eyes swiftly following every movement while the rest of him stayed motionless.

"Do you intend me harm?" I asked.

He did not reply for a long moment, and then he said, "I do not intend you harm. But that does not mean I will not harm you."

Could I get out of bed and leave the room, I wondered, or if I tried would he stop me? Should I strike him? There were, I remembered, in the monitor, back before the monitor had shut down, back in my earliest days before the corruption had spread, instructions on how to kill a person such as Horak, if *person* is the right word, in a way that would keep him dead. Unless I was getting confused with something else. I turned my attention inward, peeling back the layers to reveal the thoughts of each self, but this told me little more. *Decapitation,* I seemed to remember, *the filling of the mouth with straw,* whatever straw was, *the driving of a sharpened stick or stake through the heart,* followed by *immolation of severed head and body in separate fires.*

He said, "If I stay here too long with you, I will make you ill. I have brought the outside in with me, so to speak. I am the outside made manifest."

"Take the outside out again," I said.

"I can," he said. "I will. But to do so I must take myself outside as well. And before I do I have some things I must ask of you. Can I question you?"

"No," I said.

"No?" he said.

"Please leave," I said.

"How can I leave until I have answers to my questions?" he asked. "Shall I ask them quickly before you become ill? Or shall I ask them slowly and wait for you to die?"

When I did not respond, he proceeded to question me as if I had said yes after all.

• • •

"Was it you who cut the cables and disabled my storage?"

When I did not answer, he waited and then repeated the question. "Why do you want to know?" I asked.

"Was it you?" he asked.

"Who else is there?"

He gave a slow nod and smiled. "Yes," he said. "Exactly. Who else is there?"

When, some time later, I realized this was not a purely rhetorical question, I answered: "No one else."

• • •

For a time he was not there. I felt my limbs heavy and could not get up. I even slept, my eyes open. When I stirred again, I felt a burning in my chest, and when I peeled my shirt up I saw a bloody handprint where he had touched me.

I tried to get up and leave the bedroom. I managed to get my feet out of the bed and onto the floor, but when I tried to walk, I found my legs becoming tangled one with another and I fell, pitching flat onto the floor. From there I could not get up.

• • •

I do not know how much time went by. But time did go by, I am almost sure of it. And it was not a dream, I am almost sure of that, too.

• • •

When I awoke again, I was back in the bed, only at first I did not recognize I was in the bed because I was also in a suit. Helmet affixed. Horak was there, looking a little less haggard, tapping gently on my faceplate. I turned my head and saw the chest in which the suit had been stored. The lock on it had been broken, torn off as if by some tremendous force.

When he saw I was awake, he smiled.

"You'll be safer like this," he said. "We can talk longer. Even so, to be safe, when I leave you should wear the suit for several days, and for even a few days after that do not touch anything that you see me touch."

I could feel a heat on my wrist, along my sides, on one forearm: where he must have grabbed hold of me to force me into the suit. I imagined the blood seeping from my skin there, and there, and there, and there.

He said to me, "What happened to the others?"

"Dead," I said. "All dead."

"Why?"

"Not enough material. I was the last one formed. Now,

what are we to form the next one with? What body are the selves to populate next?"

"Formed? Populated?" he asked. "What do you mean?"

I gestured toward my tablature and described its operation best I could. He went over to it and observed it more closely, bringing his eyes close to it, running his finger along its runnel. Then he shook his head.

"That is not the use for which this is intended," he said.

I shrugged. How did I know its intention? And what did intention matter in a world such as this, on the verge of dying out?

He came closer to me, squinting. He took hold of my helmet and turned it, then moved his body to block the light shining on it and into my eyes, and peered in.

"There is not room enough in the head," he said. "They should never have done this." He rapped on my faceplate. Inside, many pairs of eyes opened. "Do you feel that?" he asked. "Where does the sound catch? What part of your skull?"

"I don't understand the question," I said. Through the filter of the suit my voice came out sounding flattened, inhuman. More like the voice of the monitor than the voice of a person.

"Do you have headaches?" Horak asked. "Does your skull sometimes feel like it is prepared to split open?"

I ignored him.

"Wouldn't you like to be rid of all these personalities?" he asked. "All these 'selves'"—he made crooking motions with his fingers—"imposed upon the organic matter of your brain?"

But if they do not abide within me, where will they go? They cannot reside within the monitor, not now, cannot be stored in that or other ways without danger of corruption. Even with me there is danger of corruption, but less so. Or at least, so Wollem led me to believe, more chance of them someday finding a more permanent home.

But why would Wollem know? He knew little more than I—much less, in fact, considering that his head was not crowded with selves. And yet Wollem was bipedal, an individual thought process enmeshed in a body. In that sense, he met the monitor's qualifications for being a person more thoroughly than I do myself.

• • •

Horak was gone. I was there, still, on the bed, still in my suit. The places where his hands had touched me had stopped aching but were painful and sore, and felt wet within the suit, too, and I imagined the blood vessels ruptured on the surface and the skin weakened too, the cellular walls collapsing, blood beading on the surface of my skin to form the outline of his touch, the contour of a finger, a palm—a different sort of recording of another self. My chest, too, was still wet with blood, slow to heal. But how slow I did not yet know.

I was not sure how many days had gone by. I tried to sit up, to pull myself up, but it was too much effort, too exhausting. I raised my head and let it fall back. Here I was, just one of me, trying not only to control and move the body we occupied but to keep control of the others, to keep them subdued, half asleep, lulled, safe.

• • •

After a while, I began to feel ill. I tried again to get up but still could not. My skin felt like it needed to be shed, buzzing and itching as it was, and I could feel my muscles jerking and moving on their own accord, without me having anything to do with them.

I vomited a pale spume that clung to the inside of the faceplate and slowly began to slip down the faceplate's curve, dripping off and into my ears and hair. The smell of it was acrid in my nose. I tried to get up and this time managed to move enough to roll off the bed and finish facedown on the floor.

Help me I cried. *Horak, help me!* Though I suspected that it was Horak himself, his contact with me, that had put me in this position. I say *I cried,* but I don't know that I even managed to speak. *Help me,* I cried again, or at least thought.

In my head, pairs of eyes started clicking open like the dead and flinty eyes of dolls. They watched me, attentive. I turned my gaze inward and watched them in turn, and saw faces form around them, mouths too, and saw them become substantial, or seemingly so.

You want me to help you? said one, his jaw slipping awkwardly as he said it, his voice not quite matching the movements of his mouth.

I said nothing to him. I remained motionless.

I can help you, he said. *If you let me. Will you let me?*

I am willing to help you, he said, after a time. *But what I want to know is this: what are you willing to do for me?*

IV

I do not understand this body exactly, and yet it is good to have a body again, even a poisoned and perhaps dying one, rather than be subsumed in that half-sleep and woozy oblivion, tucked into the back of a head. Now that I am at the front of the head, residing just behind the eyes, there is nothing that will drive me back again.

It was some effort to stand, but even the pain of that felt new to me and was something that I welcomed, at least at first. The suit stank inside from where he had been sick—where I had been sick, I suppose I should say. Once I was on my feet, I unbuckled his faceplate and tugged it trembling upward until it detached and cleared the top of his head and clattered to the ground. The body was sick and I was still learning to properly manipulate the arms, so this was not a simple matter. The rest of the suit I stripped out of over time and, in the end, was left trembling and exhausted, leaning against a wall.

After a while, I managed to make my way to a mirror and stare into it. It was strange to see someone who resembled me so closely but who was not me. Not exactly.

Strange to see within the face the struggle between the mannerisms that had long possessed it and those that came more naturally to me. The flesh will learn to be subject to me. The features were roughly the same, both of us having been fabricated of the same material upon the same tablature, but there were different marks on the body, different blemishes and scars. On the chest, just in the middle, was a birthmark that resembled nothing so much as a hand. On one wrist and one arm and one leg I found patches of skin that were damaged, the skin sloughing away at a touch to reveal underneath a layer of more sensitive dermis speckled with pus and blood, an unpleasant smell to the flesh.

And stranger still to be alone, just one of me. Before, there were always at least two, myself and Vagus, one thought process spread over two bodies. But Vagus was gone now. At first I thought him there still, lodged like a scrap of meat between the teeth of this new brain, but like such a scrap, he had been gnawed and rended, and the little that was left of him was in no shape to be anyone at all.

• • •

The warren was much as it had been before, more or less. There were fewer stores, things had been moved, but all in all it was as I remembered it. I found a can of something and opened it and ate it. I found an old corridor that had black mushrooms fruiting in it.

"Monitor," I inquired, "are these mushrooms edible?"

But there must have been a short in the ports in that corridor, for the monitor did not respond, perhaps did not hear me.

I broke one off and ate it, and when I did not grow sick, I ate several more.

• • •

"Monitor," I asked once I was back in the open warren. "How many years have passed since the death of Vagus?"

There was no response.

I repeated the question, and when there still was no answer, I began to become worried.

• • •

It took me several hours to locate the power unit of the monitor. When I did, I found it deluminant, the system offline. Restarting the monitor had not been part of my assigned tasks, was not part of my purpose. Vagus had been trained in this, but what was left of Vagus was maddened and torqued and would be of little help. I could not risk giving him control of the body, for I did not know what he would do with it and I was certain he would not surrender it back to me once he was done.

Though Vagus had never had to restart the monitor, he had had to simulate doing so at regular intervals, and sometimes I had watched him. I fixed my memory of this in my head, the image of his back as he bent over the panel, and tried to imagine too by the flinching of his shoulder blades and the glimpse I had of one of his arms which controls he was touching and what he was doing with them.

• • •

For several hours I experimented, pressing first this and then that, waiting a long moment, listening to the sounds coming from the monitor, throwing what I eventually determined was the kill switch and starting over if I feared something was going wrong.

At one moment I thought I had disabled the monitor for good when it refused to even begin to luminate, but no, after a brief period of inactivity, of failing to respond to the manipulation of any of the controls, it started responding again. And a few minutes after that, it spoke for the first time:

Enter password, the monitor said.

Password? I wondered. I turned my eyes inward, as I

had often seen that other do, and peered back deeper into the brain, waiting for my gaze to adjust, slumbering faces slowly forming out of darkness. I scrutinized them carefully. Wollem was not there, apparently not having been preserved, and I felt a little grief to know that the person we had created to follow after us was forever lost. There was X—I did not know his name but knew that it would start with X, just as Vagus and I knew to name Wollem something beginning with a W, to continue the sequence. X was the most recent, the closest to the surface; there was nobody beyond him. And yet he was folded in on himself, damaged. I reached out and parted his skull and stared inside, but either he knew nothing of this password or couldn't reveal it, or wouldn't.

I touched each of the others lightly in turn, stirring their slumber, and learned nothing.

X seems not to have knowledge of a password, I thought. *Wollem has not been preserved so cannot be asked. The next people in line would be myself and Vagus. I have no knowledge of a password. But perhaps Vagus does.*

Did he? I examined again the twisted fragment that was all that was left of Vagus and reached slowly toward it, and then drew back as if afraid of being stung.

Vagus, I said.

His single eyelid squinched, tightened, but the eye did not open.

Vagus, I said again, *wake up, brother. I need you.*

The eyelid opened to reveal a milky blind orb behind. The head formed, swelling out of the darkness—or not formed exactly, for that would be to suggest a coherent coming-together of disparate parts. No, what happened, the terrible thing that happened, was that these parts refused to come together: a single milky eye, a fragment of tooth, one cheek planed smooth on one side, a bit of neck, a tuft of hair. In the place of the mouth was just a hole, but less the kind of hole you could fall into, a hole with depth, and more just a circle of profound, featureless darkness, like a scrap of fuligin.

Vagus, I said, *if you can hear me, blink your eye.*

After a long moment of inactivity, the eye blinked. Or wavered. Did something that could be interpreted as a blink anyway, if only vaguely.

The monitor is down, I said. *Vagus, what is the password.*

A long hesitation and that same wavering gesture. I waited for something to follow it. Nothing did.

Vagus, I said, *tell me the password. Please.*

I saw the hole that resided in the place of his mouth and much of his lower face quiver. Out of it came a horrible noise, nothing comprehensible, an odd and terrible cross between moaning and gnashing of teeth. It filled me with fear. All around Vagus, the others' eyes began to snap open and fill with rough panic, and they too were moaning or giving little shouts and trying, in the confined and impossible space of the skull, to get away from him.

The moaning lowered in pitch and became a deafening rumbling. Before I knew what I was doing, I had opened my own mouth within my skull and was screaming myself, and with the scream came a tongue of flame that licked at Vagus's face. A moment later he was on fire within my skull, and then it had consumed him, and where he had been was an annealed and shiny patch of brain, still stinking of smoke, a dead portion, a new grave.

And so I am a murderer. I have killed my own other self, his reproduction within my head, for no reason, or little reason, and gained nothing by it.

• • •

I began trying possibilities. I was like Vagus, just as Vagus was like me. I knew how he thought, just as he, while he was still alive, knew how I thought, and if anyone could decipher the workings of his mind sufficiently to luck upon the password he might have used, it was me.

I tried things. I tried *password*. I tried *monitor*. I tried *warren*. I tried *Unnr*, the name of the one who had come directly before my brother and me. And then I tried *Uttr*, the name of the other one who came directly before us. None of it worked.

I tried other things. I cast my eyes around and tried the word for every object my eyes encountered. *Suit* and *rope* and *knife* and *wall. Mushroom,* I tried, and *room,* and *arm bone. Food can* and *broom* and . . . On and on. None of it worked.

• • •

I went to the mirror and regarded my own reflection—which was not my reflection exactly, but something in between what I was and what X had been. And then, in looking at it, I moved my face to make it something else. I summoned up Vagus, remade my flesh and lineaments, the slackness of my jaw, the tightness of my brow, to resemble him. In the end, I did not have Vagus exactly, but I did not have myself either. And X was all but completely gone, the merest suspicion of him there, the rest of him banished from the surface and hidden deep within.

"Hello, Vagus," I said.

Hello.

"Will you help me?" I asked.

Of course I will, he said. Or someone said. And that someone wasn't me. Or not exactly.

"A password," I said. "What would you have chosen?"

For a long time we stared at one another. He opened

his mouth to speak and then just as quickly closed it again. And then said, mouth still closed, *Why did you kill me?*

It is impossible he is speaking, I told myself. *This is a game that, despite only having just begun, has gone on too long. You should turn away.*

But I spoke. "You were already dead," I claimed. "I merely buried you."

You were the one I loved best, he said. *Why would you kill me? Did you not love me as well as I loved you? Who did you love better?*

Shuddering, I turned away.

• • •

They were all awake, had been since Vagus had begun to speak. They were agitated and anxious, and I could hear them muttering, repeating bits and scraps of the words Vagus had used.

"Quiet," I said, and for a moment they subsided. But, quickly, their voices rose again.

I tried to ignore them, but I could not. I hissed at them to stop. I picked up a pry bar that was lying on the ground and threatened to pound the body's head bloody with it and force them out, and myself along with them. *There is nowhere to go,* I told them. *The monitor will not take you, I won't be able to take you, that will be the end of you.*

And then, instead of pounding my head bloody, I took the pry bar to the monitor and attempted to break it apart.

It was only later, lying on the ground, having failed to break the monitor, flakes of its casing scattered about me, the screen scratched but unbroken, the pry bar beside me, that I realized what the password must be.

I uttered my name, the name of the one he loved best. *Vigus.*

Password accepted, the monitor said. *System initiated.*

• • •

Monitor, I said, *how many years have passed since the death of Vigus?*

For a moment, the monitor whirred. And then: *Define Vigus,* it said.

I will lie here just a little longer. I will catch my breath. I will rest just for a moment. And then I will stand and query the monitor, determine how it is malfunctioning, and see what hope, if any, there is left for us.

V

For hours, days, years perhaps, I was a trapped in a dream, slowly suffocating. Sensations, when they came, were muted, distant, less as if I was experiencing them and more as if someone else experiencing them was describing them to me. I could feel my mouth and sometimes the lids of my eyes, but when I moved my hands and fingers, it was as if I were moving them through a liquid just as resistant as they were and feeling nothing at all.

Something in my head still nags me, and I will not look too closely at it. Now that I can see things, can feel things again around and outside me, why would I turn my gaze inward?

• • •

I have all the usual appendages. I am doubly legged and doubly armed, just as I remembered. My face does not look exactly as I remember it looking, and this perhaps is due to my having dreamt too long. I am not certain what has been done to me. I do not remember this body as my body, and my movements within it are clumsy and ill-remembered. But it is the only body I have.

• • •

My last memories, the last clear ones anyway, were of something else, another body, another place. Or not another body exactly since it was so close to this one, a near-copy of it. I was being led to the tablature by my twin, or I was leading my twin to the tablature—something is unclear on that score. I was taking Unnr—unless it was Uttr I was taking and I was Unnr and then . . .

That's odd. Surely I know who I am? And yet both names sound familiar to me, as if I could wear either or both at once.

Something is quite wrong.

• • •

"Monitor," I said, "am I Unnr or am I Uttr?"

Move closer to the aperture and raise your head, said the monitor.

I did so, and held still. It observed me for a long time.

The question cannot be answered in these terms, it said.

Please rephrase.

I thought for a moment. "Am I Unnr?" I asked. "Yes or no."

No, it said without hesitation.

"I am Uttr, then," I said.

No.

No? Something was wrong with the monitor. It was malfunctioning, unable to apprehend the information coming through its aperture. The aperture, I saw, regarding it more closely, had become scratched somehow.

I could feel a pressure in my head. I ignored it.

"Where is Unnr?" I asked.

Dead, it said.

"And Uttr?"

Dead.

"Then," I said, wondering even as I asked if it was in fact a question it was wise to ask, "who am I?"

You do not have a name, it said. *You have only a letter, the next letter in the sequence. The one who came before you could think of no name to give you, and he saw no point in the end to giving you a name at all. He failed in his purpose, insofar as that purpose was to give you a name.*

"What is my letter?"

X.

• • •

And yet I have no knowledge of X, none at all. I remember myself as Uttr, or Unnr, or, sometimes, a strange combination of the two, as if somehow the personality of one of us has become mixed or confused or partially overwritten with the personality of the other. I have no memory of the pair starting with V that must have followed me, followed Uttr, or Unnr. Or of the pair starting with W that must have followed them. Or of the other X that must have come along with me, with this body, for we always come in pairs.

• • •

"And Tore?" I asked the monitor. "And Ture?"

Dead, it said.

"Recently?" I asked.

No, it said.

• • •

Perhaps I am neither Unnr nor Uttr but am someone else after all, someone later, as the monitor suggests. Or perhaps the monitor is broken. I can see on the floor around it small pieces of plastic that have been chipped from its casing, and a large scratch is on the screen. If it shows signs of wear on the outside, would not its inner systems show wear as well? Which is more likely, that my memories are faulty or that something is wrong with the monitor?

No, I cannot think myself as other than a U. It does not matter what the truth is. What matters is how it feels.

VI

"Monitor," we say, "how many years until it is safe to go outside again?"

It will not be possible in your lifetime, it says.

"Monitor," we say, "please answer the question."

There is not sufficient data to precisely answer the question.

Perhaps the monitor is wrong. Perhaps it will, in the end, be safe for us to leave, or if not for us, for those who come after us: for the Vs, the Ws, the Xs, the Ys, and the Zs.

• • •

And what will we do when we reach the end of our alphabet? Will we move beyond it, invent new letters, new systems of designation, to mark those who come after? Or will we circle viciously back to begin again?

• • •

It is time for us to create our descendants. We set about our task, remembering how we were instructed by Tore and Ture. Our memory of the sequence is more vague and partial than we would like, but time has gone by and we are older; of course our memory is tarnished.

Unnr describes the sequence as he remembers it, and then, taking hold of the mouth myself, I describe it as I remember it. Between the two of us, we seem to have most of it.

We take our body and go in search of the tablature. It is where we remember it being, in the same room and in the same spot, and the squares of rust outlining its footing make it clear it has never been moved, or at least not moved in a very long time. We go from there to the preservation chamber, and though the chamber inside is fully functional, bitterly cold, it is empty. There is no material.

Perhaps there is another preservation chamber, says Uttr.

But why would there be another such chamber? There was no other chamber before, I am sure of it, and yet together we propel the body in search of it. We search through the warren for another preservation chamber and find only the rubbish and disjecta of all those who came before, the dwindling supplies, the blocked, dirt-filled passages. These latter we dig out, slowly and surely, and we cannot understand why they would have been blocked, until our shovel cuts through the wall at the back of one to reveal a glimpse of sunlight and open air.

Quickly, heart pounding, holding our breath, we retreat. We don the suit and return and fill the tunnel again, packing the dirt in tight. We return to the heart of the warren and there strip and scrub the body clean. A few hours later, we are vomiting a yellow fluid that slowly colors red. By nightfall, we are stumbling and dizzy and experiencing a great fatigue.

• • •

And now what do we do? Do we wait here, exhausted, on our bed, until we either die or heal? If we die, there will be no more hope for us; everything will end there. There will only be the monitor, damaged but attentive, waiting until its power source expires.

We cannot risk waiting until we know if we are dying or merely sick. We must, Uttr tells me, I tell Unnr, make a last effort, a final search.

"Monitor," we say from my bed, "where shall we go to find more material?"

Define: material.

"That which is needed to generate another person," we say.

Query: what do you mean by "person"?

I have that unsettling feeling of hearing something I have already heard before. And yet this is the first time I have had this conversation. We, I mean. Not I, we.

Or no, only I. For one of us is gone now, slumbering, sleeping. Where has he gone? Perhaps he will come back, perhaps not. What a strange, terrible thing to again be alone.

Query, repeats the monitor, *what do you mean by "person"?*

"What do *you* mean by person?" I ask slowly, and the words as I say them sound familiar.

It responds, *Bipedal, an individual thought process enmeshed in a body, procreated through the fertilization of an ovum by a sperm and its subsequent development in a womb.*

I think this over. There is much of what it says that I cannot understand, words that I think I should know but that I do not. "Me," I finally say. "The material to make a person like me."

The monitor's aperture opens wider as it regards me for a long time. I might think it has ceased to function were it not for the light blinking beside the aperture.

But you, it finally says. *By what definition are you a person at all?*

VII

Some time passed, a few days. Hair, when I rubbed a hand along the scalp, came away in clumps, uprooted. I forced my way out of the bed and crawled to a cache of cans. I would have eaten the contents of one but could not find the pry. I found the spigot and had a little water and vomited it up again, and then had a little more and this time kept it down.

A few more days went by and I managed to get up off the floor and make it back to the bed, rolling a can along before me, and though I did not at first have the strength to climb into the bed, eventually I did. I was weak and ill but not dead, not yet. It was not long after that that I stumbled upon the pry and opened the can and choked down its contents. Now I would either get better or have a brief moment of respite followed by sickness unto death.

How many days did I have left to me? Many? Only a few? The Ts had told me that we lived sometimes five years, sometimes a few less, sometimes a few more, depending on our exposure to the outside air. How long had I been alive? What was my purpose?

I slowly worked my way into the suit. I walked through the warren and to the seal and then passed through, coming out on the other side scrubbed and clean. There was the ladder. I put my foot on the rung and began my ascent.

• • •

The climb was difficult. Often, I found myself stopping and wrapping my arms around the rung in front of my face, waiting for my dizziness to subside. It never subsided entirely, but a few moments of rest, a few careful breaths, and I could move upward again without the risk of falling.

I crawled off the ladder and pushed my way through the second seal and out into the world beyond. The light was brighter than any I had ever seen, or at least that I remembered having seen, and it took some time for my eyes to adjust. Not far from the seal was a structure made of materials not dissimilar to those found in the warren, and I went toward this, having no clear goal in mind. Perhaps I would get lucky, I told myself, and find the material I needed here, close by. Then I could go down again almost immediately before the air leaked too thoroughly through my suit and poisoned me enough to kill me.

But as I came closer, I became less optimistic. The metal door of the structure hung loose and open, as if it had been abandoned or even raided. Inside, there was only some kind of storage chamber, but less the sort that would hold the cylinders that would contain material and more the sort meant to store a full-grown person. It was empty. There were, I saw, peering in, straps by which the wrists, ankles and chest of the person stored could be secured. The cabling at the back of the chamber had been cleanly cut, making the chamber no longer functional.

I opened all lockers and cabinets but found nothing useful.

And so I left. I stepped out of the structure and into the world outside. I let my eyes wander, looking for something that I might walk toward, but it seemed as if the same red-gray waste stretched indifferently in every direction.

I closed my eyes and spun around until the dizziness became unbearable, and then I opened them and took a lurching step forward. This was the direction to which I consigned my fate.

• • •

I walked for several hours, or at least what I would judge to be several hours. I have no way of judging time here except by the motion of the sun, and not knowing the particulars of this place, I do not know how to judge that with any accuracy.

I only stopped because I could go no farther. My legs ached and my dizziness had so intensified that I had to lie flat on the ground. Everything still spun around me, but I could bear it better when I was anchored by more than just the soles of my feet.

I lay there, breathing in and out, waiting for the dizziness to subside. How long had it been since I had eaten? I found it curious that nowhere in my memory of the last few weeks did food feature at all. Perhaps, I told myself, this was what was causing my dizziness, rather than a more serious condition.

I watched the sun hesitate beside a mountain peak and then, finally, slip behind it and subside. The air grew dark until it was as dark as it can be in the warren with all light extinguished except the emergency indicators, and then it grew darker still. I could see nothing at all. Even if I raised my gloved hand in front of my faceplate, I could not see its fingers. My body grew cold and I began to shiver.

I do not know how many hours went by. I know so little, I now realize, about life outside the warren. The little I have been told seems largely to have been warnings intended to keep me within the warren.

But some hours went by. I am sure about that, even if I am not certain how many. Maybe a dozen, maybe less. As I grew colder, I imagine the hours went slower, but without any kind of chronometer this is more an impression than a certainty. In the end, light began to leak back into the world and, half-frozen, still nauseous, I regained my feet and continued walking.

The sun, again, never rose high in the sky but mounted just a little and then rode a slow arc before descending again. I walked all day, stopping periodically to rest or quell my dizziness. I vomited and wallowed in the stench of the bile. I saw things: an endlessly flat landscape, dust so powdery and fine it clung everywhere to my suit, rocks that I saw less than stumbled on. There was no sign of habitation, and when I turned, just before the sun departed, and looked behind me, I saw no sign of the warren, despite the flatness of the ground.

• • •

I lay on the ground, trying to sleep, until I started shivering. I bore that as long as I could and then stood and continued to walk, fighting wave after wave of nausea. When I vomited, nothing came out, but it was long before I could stop retching.

At what point, I wondered, lying on the ground again

in the darkness, *do I decide that I am going in the wrong direction? At what point do I decide there is no material to be found and simply return to the warren to die?*

• • •

The sky lightened. I regained my feet and stumbled forward. The landscape was the same as it had been, except for places where the dust was not dust at all but sand. Another half-morning's walk, and there were what looked like veins of glass running through the sand, strange solid patches, as if the desert floor had been subject to great heat.

There is no point in going on, I thought. I turned around to look behind me to see if now, somehow, I might catch a glimpse of the warren, but I still saw nothing. I was not exactly sure where to go. Which meant perhaps there was no point in turning back either.

What is this place we are in? Have we always been here or did we come here for some reason now lost to us? Why do I not know the answer to these questions?

• • •

Indecisive, I scanned the horizon, and this time thought I saw a slight disruption at some distance, almost too far away to be seen. What was it? It was too far away to say if it was indeed anything at all. But whether it was actually something or simply a mirage, it was enough to drive me forward.

• • •

Only in the declining light of the sun did I become certain: yes, there was something there, glittering, catching light, and a jagged shape, too, something projecting beyond the flatness of the desert floor. The veins of glass had become thicker now, winding together at times to form flat, smooth patches that were almost like the remnants of what the monitor had instructed me was a road. But how strange, to have a road made of glass.

I kept up my crippled pace, stopping when I had to, trying to ignore the smell of vomit and bile sharp in my nostrils, the dryness of my tongue, my parched throat and lips. I tried my best to direct myself in the waning light. When the darkness fell, I kept walking, trying to stay on course as best I could—I was so weak I did not dare to wait through the night and try to set off again. No, better to keep going, keep walking, as long as I could, and try to arrive at wherever I was going before I died.

In the pitch darkness, I stumbled several times and fell, and once in falling struck my faceplate so hard against a lump of glass that it tolled like a bell, but did not break.

There was, too, I could now hear through the ports embedded on the outside of my helmet in lieu of ears, a low and near-constant sound, something like an endless moan. At first, I thought I might have injured one or both ports, but as I continued to walk, the moan grew louder.

When darkness at last began to vanish, the sound had grown very loud, so loud that I had to decrease the volume of the ports.

By daylight, I could see where it was coming from. In the middle of the flat, desert landscape was a sandy crater, a bowl-like depression, perhaps a mile across, as if, many years ago, a meteor had struck. What I had seen from a distance was simply the protrusion over the lip of the bowl of one of many vertical stones, perhaps three hundred in all.

At first, I thought them as tall as or a little taller than a man, but as the light improved and I drew closer, I realized they were a great deal taller than that. In the middle of the afternoon, when I found myself standing among them, I found them four or five times my own height: massive stones, shaped apparently not by wind or erosion but by hand. And not stones exactly—or at least not merely stones, but tortured sculptures made of a material similar to basalt.

Each of these emitted the same horrible moaning

sound, almost without cease. As I approached, they began to glow slightly as well and give the appearance of vibrating, though I did not dare touch them so as to discover if they actually did vibrate. Once I was standing in the midst of them, it was difficult to know anything for certain. The sound had grown so loud that I had begun to feel it through the fabric of my suit, and even with the ports muted I found this moaning that hands had inflicted upon stone almost impossible to bear.

There was nothing for me here. We had had a good run, and now it was time for us to die out, to follow everything else here that had already gone. I turned and plodded back up the hill, but the slope, gentle though it was, combined with the looseness of the sand, thwarted me. I climbed a bit and then slipped, fell back. I stood and tried again. I made a little progress, but in the awkward suit for every two steps I made, one step was lost and sometimes more. I had to stop, panting, to rest.

And what, I thought, catching my breath, *would I gain by reaching the top?* I had no place to go, I was as good as dead. Why not die there? At least there I would have stones to moan over me as I died.

I shivered. I kept struggling upward. And in the end I would have made the top had there not been a crumbling of a lip of sand that brought me tumbling along the flow of it back nearly to where I had started.

• • •

It was there, waiting, that I found my mind beginning to diverge from itself. Part of me—several parts it seemed, full and complete in their sense of themselves, though I was careful not to regard them too closely—continued to think these same death-bound thoughts, of the relief that extinction of self and species would provide. Another part, a stubborn bit of me, struggled on. I had come down originally spilling little sand, that part told me, so there must be some places where the sand was sturdier than others, crusted together. Perhaps even places where, as in the rest of the desert, the sand had been replaced by half-formed glass.

And so, rather than climb again, I walked the perimeter of the stones just at the base of the slope. I examined the ground, testing it, looking for something more promising, deafened by the moans. My extremities tingled with the sound and I idly wondered, if I remained there long enough, would it shake me into a jelly? *Lie down and die*, the muffled chorus within me suggested, but that other me, the one currently in charge of the body that conveyed all of us, refused to give up. Instead, it kept slowly circling, looking for a way out.

And then, once again, I grew weary and dizzy, and stood there swaying and trying to keep my balance. I coughed and spattered the inside of the faceplate with a fine mist of blood. I felt my leg buckle and moved to compensate for it, suddenly veering. I would have fallen, would have gone down, perhaps for good, but my shoulder came into contact with something solid and caught me before I did.

It took me a moment to realize that I was balanced against what could only be one of the moaning statues. Upon my touch, it began to glow brighter. It was warm, even hot, and as I pulled my shoulder away I saw smoke curling up from the rubberized fabric of the shoulder where I had touched it, the material weakened but not yet breached. I could feel an ache there that spread as the seconds passed until the whole shoulder felt inflamed. And then, as quickly as it came, it passed away, leaving the fabric melted to the skin, the arm feeling like it was still on fire.

• • •

When I came conscious again, the moans had changed pitch, descending even lower, as if trying to burrow subcutaneously through me. Deep within my skull, something had changed, and I felt pair after pair of eyes snap open and then remain there attentive, glowing yellow and bloody in the dark. An image appeared on my faceplate, but it was not, I somehow perceived, an image projected onto it from outside. No, instead, I felt that what was occurring was occurring inside my head and that I was being made to see it outside of me, as if a projection, since this would unsettle me less. But in fact, since I detected the sleight of hand, it unsettled me even more.

It was the image of a young man, perhaps only two inches tall, but seeming much taller because of the image's proximity to my eyes. Somehow, though he was but an image, he seemed to possess not two dimensions but three. He wore a suit like my own—indeed, with the very same scars and marks on it, including the melted and stretched fabric at the shoulder—though unlike me he carried his helmet under one arm. He was not unlike myself in appearance—indeed, as close in appearance to me as my twin had been, perhaps closer. His visible skin was pale, slightly translucent, and he had the beginnings of a beard. He wore his hair like I wore mine, cropped short and brushed to one side, but while I brushed mine to the left side, he brushed his to the other. He had, like me, canines that jutted out slightly and deformed his lower lip.

I immediately disliked him.

When he seemed to notice me, he offered up a broad, open smile. And then he spoke with great urgency and sincerity in a language I could not remotely begin to understand.

• • •

When he finished, he remained there, as if expecting a response, flickering gently as he waited. And then, when no response was forthcoming, he again gave his same broad and empty smile and then repeated, as far as I could determine, the same speech in the same language.

"I'm sorry," I said, "I don't understand you."

Immediately, the figure flickered and vanished. Clutching my injured arm, I tried to get my feet under me and rise.

I was just giving up the attempt when he reappeared. He was dressed not in a suit this time but in a different outfit made of what I judged to be homespun cloth—something I had only seen portrayed in my early instruction from the monitor as an example of clothing that persons once wore. In all other particulars, the man was the same. When he spoke again, though his words were now in a language I understood, his mouth did not move in concord with them, as if it were still speaking the language it had first spoken.

Stranger! he said, the words either coming strong through my muted ports or arising directly within the head itself. *You must flee this place! Stranger! It is not safe here! A terrible poison resides in the air that will last for many years! This is a poison that you or your enemies created and you all are to be blamed! Shame on you! This is not a safe place! Stranger, flee!*

But I could not even move, let alone flee. I lay there in my heap on the ground. My body within the suit felt slick as if with blood. Slowly, I allowed unconsciousness to overwhelm me.

VIII

I was lying on the tablature in what was either the warren or a reasonable approximation thereof. I was wearing my suit, but the helmet had been removed. I wasn't sure if I had just come back into the warren or was about to go out.

I tried to get up but could not. Something held me in place, and it took me some time to realize that I had been strapped down. Intravenous lines ran into my arms, and hanging from the pole at the top of the tablature was a bag filled with a yellowish fluid.

"Hello?" I said weakly. "Hello?"

I tested the straps but they were firm and without flaw.

"Monitor," I said, "Loosen these straps."

Enter override, the monitor said.

"I don't need a goddamn override," I said. "Loosen the straps."

Enter override, the monitor repeated.

I had no override. "Monitor—" I started to say, when I was interrupted.

"It's no use," a dim voice said. "It doesn't understand."

I turned my head and it was only then that I saw, in the corner of the room, a man.

He was long-legged and gangly, thin-fingered and horse-faced: much different from me. I did not know him, had never met him, but I recognized his appearance from instruction with the monitor: either this was Horak or it was a man who resembled him in every particular and was thus his descendant.

"Who are you?" I asked him.

"You know who I am," he said. "It was you who removed me from storage."

And yet I had no memory of doing so.

"Why don't you sit closer?" I asked. "Why are you all the way across the room?"

He shook his head. "It is safer for you," he said.

Safer how? I wondered. "What's wrong with it?" I asked, gesturing with my chin to the monitor.

He shrugged. "Faulty memory," he said. "Among other things. Had I known, I wouldn't have strapped you in—though without that, you probably would have pulled out the tubes, so maybe I would have regardless. But what's done is done." He gestured down to an ax leaning against the wall beside him. "Before I go, I'll cut you loose."

"Why not cut me loose now?" I asked.

"I have a few questions," he claimed.

"I'm happy to answer them. Cut off the straps."

"I thought it better to keep you tethered until you had answered them."

"Why wouldn't I stay in one place on my own?"

He looked at me curiously. "Perhaps that's something that you should tell me."

"Excuse me?"

"Since both other times when I attempted to question you, you fled."

And yet I had, and still have, no memory of these times either, and even looking back at these pages, I see I have not recorded them. It is as if I have lost touch with my own mind, my own body.

• • •

"Shall we start with an easy one?" Horak asked. "What is your name?"

For a long, horrifying moment, I didn't know. There just wasn't a name there. Even though he was at a distance, I could feel his gaze resting steadily upon me, like the pressing of a thumb.

"I don't know," I said. "I can't remember."

"Not good enough," he said, forming a basket with his hands. "Try again."

And there was something in his voice that made me

feel I had to. I searched the room, hoping for something to jog my memory, but there was nothing.

And then, suddenly, it came to me.

"X," I said.

"X?" he said. "X is not a name, it's a letter."

"Wollem was to name me," I said, the memories coming back thicker now. "Something starting with X to maintain the sequence. But if this was his purpose he failed in it and never named me. He never gave me more than a letter."

"Very good," he said. "Perhaps X really is your name, if we can call it a name. But why is it that each time I've asked you your name, you've come up with a different one?"

I am X, I am almost certain of it. I am not, as I apparently variously told Horak, Vigus, Vagus, Unnr, Uttr, Tore, Ture, or any number of others that came earlier. And yet, why would I give Horak these names instead of my own?

What is wrong with me?

• • •

He said to me, "What brought you to this place?"

"The warren?" I said. "I've always lived here, as long as I've existed. I was made here."

"You call it the warren?" he asked. "Why?"

"That's what I was taught to call it."

"Who taught you this?"

"Wollem," I said. "Who else?"

"And who taught Wollem?" he asked.

"Either Vigus or Vagus," I said. "I do not know which. This is how we relay information, from an older mouth to a younger ear, with each of us being told what the others before him knew."

"And where did it all begin?" he asked.

"Begin?" I said. "With the founder, of course. Aarskog, also known by some as Aarskog-Scott."

"And who came before Aarskog?"

"No one came before Aarskog," I said, a little offended. "He was the founder. He was the first."

He pulled himself forward a little in his chair. "Who taught Aarskog?" he asked.

"Nobody," I said.

"Then how did he know?"

"He just knew," I claimed, though in truth I had never considered the question before and did not want to consider it now.

• • •

Horak said to me, "What are you, exactly?"

I tugged against the straps. "Cut me loose," I said.

"No," he said. "Not until you answer my questions. What are you exactly?"

I responded, "I'm human, just like you."

"Not just like me," he said.

"No," I conceded, "maybe not."

"How do we differ?"

"We are both bipedal," I said.

"That's how we are the same," he said.

"I don't care to talk about this," I said.

"Look at you," he said, ignoring this. For the first time, he stood and approached me. As he came closer, I could almost feel the heat radiating off him. I shrank back a little, as far as the straps would allow.

"That's right," he said. "I don't mean to hurt you, but you should be afraid of me." He reached out and I saw the flash of steel that he had in his hands, but with my arms strapped had no way of avoiding it or parrying it. He slashed deep and through the fabric of my suit and spread the lips of the slash wide.

"Lift your head," he said. "Tell me what you see."

"No," I said.

"You see here," he said, and pointed down at some part of my chest that, because I refused to lift my head, I could not see. "That patch of black there, just below the skin?" He reached out again, and when I felt first a pressure and then a rush of pain, I knew he must have sliced into it. "It's been dead for some time, that patch, and the tissue around it as well."

"A body is just material," I said.

"What does that mean, 'material'?" he asked. "The body has been dead for some time, but you are still animate. Why?"

"A body is just material," I repeated.

"What are you?" he said, his voice rising. "Tell me! What are you, really? What have you done with all the rest of us? Why have I changed? Why am I the only one still alive?"

I had no answers to these questions, which struck me as entirely the wrong questions to ask. And so, despite his anger, despite his prodding, I remained silent.

• • •

After a while, Horak was reduced to silence. For a moment, he put his hands around my throat and choked me, but when he remembered what his touch did to my skin, he pulled his hands off and backed slowly away, finally calming and settling in his chair in the corner. He sat there for a long time, running his hands through his hair, gathering his thoughts.

"You still insist you are human," he said.

"I am bipedal," I said.

"You are not what you think you are," he said.

He bowed his head and stared at the floor, rubbing his face with his hands. I watched him do this for a long time and then asked, "Are you done with your questions?"

"This body of yours is dying," he said. "It is already dead." He stood up and approached me with the ax. I thought that finally he intended to release me, and so I moved my head a little to one side and watched, placidly, as he raised the ax.

"What happens to a human when he is cut?" he asked.

"Excuse me?"

"Surely, this machine called a monitor has taught you this information. Is it that you simply can't recall?"

"*A human bleeds,*" I quoted.

"What color is this blood?"

I had learned nothing about this from the monitor, but I had seen my own blood, had vomited it out, and sometimes watched it escape my body after I had been hurt or injured. "Yellow," I said. "Growing deeper in shade when exposed to air."

"This is the same with the air inside of what you call the warren as without?"

I thought for a moment and then shook my head. "I don't know," I said. "I have bled in the suit and in the warren but never to my memory outside."

He nodded. "And you are, you claim, a human?"

"I am a person," I said, and nodded.

"And you claim that these two things are the same? To be a human and to be a person?"

I thought back, trying to remember what, if anything, the monitor had told me about that. But it had, as far as I could recall, told me nothing. Perhaps I simply had not asked the correct questions.

I remembered, though, the monitor's query: *What do you mean by "person"?* As if it were willing, for whatever reason, to accept my definition of what a person was, to modify its own. If I had claimed to be a human rather than a person, would its answer have been different?

Too often, I told myself, that is the problem: we do not know to ask the right questions.

"Why not?" I said at last. "Why would 'human' not be the same as 'person'?"

"You are a person," said Horak. "At least by some definitions. Considering there is no longer a legal authority in this place to make a judgment on the matter, we will accept that without debate. But you are not human."

"Don't be ridiculous," I said.

"If you were human, you could live in the air outside without damage," he said. "Just like me. If you were human, you would be like me."

I began to grow angry. "Who is to say that I'm not the

one who is human and you who is not?"

"Blood is to say," he said, and with a sudden powerful movement of the ax he struck through the wrist of the suit and cut off my hand.

• • •

It was just as I had told him, and put, I thought at first, the lie to his initial statement that I was not human. A pale yellow fluid pumped out of me, rapidly congealing into a sticky paste. In its glove, the hand flexed its fingers and struggled to right itself, and managed through a series of contortions to worm backward until it was in the pool of paste. I moved the stump of my wrist just a little until the hand and the wrist touched and sealed again together. I flexed my fingers and felt them shoot through with pain. I would have to be careful with the hand for a few hours, and it might have adhered crookedly to the wrist—it was difficult to get the right seal with my arm strapped down—but soon it would be as good, or almost as good, as new.

"There," I said, "you see? Human after all."

• • •

"Watch," said Horak, and bared his own wrist. This he did

not cut off but simply slid the blade along gently, making a shallow cut. A reddish substance immediately filled the wound and slowly began to leak down the wrist. Unlike my blood, this did not congeal properly but remained liquid for far longer than was optimal to prevent infection.

"What are you?" I asked.

"I'm human," he said. "What does that make you?"

Though I was willing to agree that only one of us was human, I was not willing to agree with him about which one of us was. Perhaps he had been human once, but he was no longer—even with the fragmented archive that the monitor had, I knew that much. If one of us was to be considered human, that person should be me.

• • •

When I continued to argue, he said, "Shall we ask the monitor?"

"You've already told me that the monitor is broken," I said. "Who knows what madness it might offer? Whether it said one or both or neither of us, it would prove nothing."

He nodded. "Why does it matter if you are a human or not as long as you are a person?" he asked. And though I didn't have a good answer to that question, I still felt, in some way, that it *did* matter.

"If not a human," I asked, "then what am I?" And,

when he could give me no adequate response, I thought that yes, I was the one who was human, not he. But if our situations had been reversed and I had been the one trying to answer the question about him, wouldn't I have been as unsuccessful as he?

And yet, I kept arguing.

• • •

In the end, he sighed.

"I was hoping to avoid this," he said. He left the room. When he came back he was carrying a mirror. He propped it up on a table near the tablature and then bent so he could confirm that I saw myself in it.

"Keep your eyes open," he said, moving his hand higher on the ax handle so that he could hold it balanced with one hand. Then, taking hold of a clump of my hair, he struck off my head.

I was surprised by this, but even more surprised when I realized that though my head was severed, I could still see out of its eyes. He had lifted me by the hair and was pointing my face at the mirror, and I could see the lips of the head moving in the reflection of the glass.

"Look at the neck," he said, and looking down I could see, among the pool of yellow fluid where the spinal column should be, a vague feathering dark strand or rope that undulated for a moment and then, as I watched, knotted in upon itself and slipped back down the neck. And then, very suddenly, I realized that for once I was alone, that there were no other selves half-slumbering and waiting to wake up completely, that I was alone in the head while the rest of us, the other selves, were elsewhere, in the body.

For a moment, I felt ecstatic, and then, quickly, felt very lonely.

"Put us back," I said. It came out as a vague, airless rush but either Horak understood me or he had intended to put the head back all along.

He carefully replaced me, and a moment later I felt head and body come back together and the rushing back into my consciousness of those other, slumbering selves. Then Horak with four blows severed the straps that bound me and extended the haft of the ax to me to help me to stand.

He directed me again before the mirror, pushing me forward with the butt of the ax handle, and stood near me as I surveyed myself. Something was wrong, a little off, but it wasn't until I had looked at myself for a long time that I realized what it was, that my head had been replaced crooked, just a little askew.

"So you don't forget," said Horak. And then he turned and left the warren.

IX

There is much I do not understand. Why for instance Horak felt some obligation to reveal to me what he saw as the truth about myself before departing the warren and climbing again into the waste. How it was that he found me and brought me back to the warren, if indeed it was he who did so. What, now that I know the truth—if it is indeed the truth and not some elaborate ruse on Horak's part—am I to do with this information? I still do not have material from which to mold another person to follow me. The air outside is poison, the monitor seems at best faulty. Everything points to an end. I myself, despite my apparent resilience in regard to axes, will not last forever. And if Horak's games have not killed me, they have nonetheless doubtless considerably shortened the span of my already-short life—if my exposure to the outer air has not killed me already. It may be that I am, in a sense, already dead and just waiting to realize it.

The materials around me, the records of the monitor, the inscribed selves stored within me, are all in the process of decaying and falling apart. Without material, nothing remains for me. I have no purpose. Even the writing of this record is an effort not likely to be completed, for, purposeless as I am, what is to stop me from running to meet my own death? From one day simply abandoning the warren, passing through the first seal and the second seal and setting foot without suit or faceplate in the waste, my body quickly dying, burning off personality after personality until all that remains is a blistered and lifeless corpse?

About the Author

BRIAN EVENSON is the author of a dozen books of fiction, most recently the story collection *A Collapse of Horses*. His collection *Windeye* (Coffee House Press 2012) and novel *Immobility* (Tor 2012) were both finalists for a Shirley Jackson Award. His novel *Last Days* won the American Library Association's award for Best Horror Novel of 2009. His novel *The Open Curtain* (Coffee House Press 2006) was a finalist for an Edgar Award and an International Horror Guild Award.

TOR·COM

Science fiction. Fantasy. The universe.

And related subjects.

*

More than just a publisher's website, *Tor.com* is a venue for **original fiction, comics,** and **discussion** of the entire field of SF and fantasy, in all media and from all sources. Visit our site today—and join the conversation yourself.

CPSIA information can be obtained
at www.ICGtesting.com
Printed in the USA
LVOW11s2100031116
511538LV00003B/201/P